WELCOME TO

Beast Quest

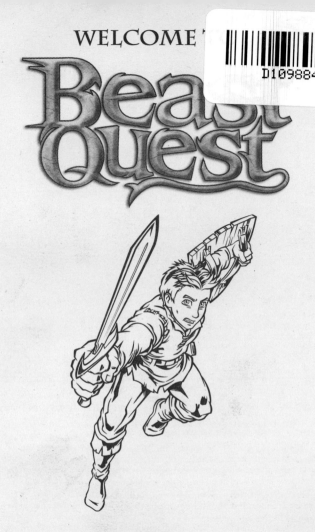

Collect the special coins in this book.
You will earn one gold coin for
every chapter you read.

Once you have finished all the chapters,
find out what to do with your gold coins at
the back of the book.

With special thanks to Michael Ford

For Alex McAteer

www.beastquest.co.uk

ORCHARD BOOKS

First published in Great Britain in 2009 by The Watts Publishing Group
This edition published in 2015

1 3 5 7 9 10 8 6 4 2

Text © 2009 Beast Quest Limited.
Cover illustrations by Steve Sims
© Beast Quest Limited 2009
Inside illustrations by Ovi@KJA-artists.com © Beast Quest Limited 2009

Beast Quest is a registered trademark of Beast Quest Limited
Series created by Beast Quest Limited, London

A CIP catalogue record for this book is available from the British Library.

ISBN 978 1 40834 822 2

Printed and bound by CPI Group (UK) Ltd, Croydon, CR0 4YY

The paper and board used in this book are made from wood from responsible sources
Orchard Books
An imprint of Hachette Children's Group
Part of The Watts Publishing Group Limited
Carmelite House, 50 Victoria Embankment, London EC4Y 0DZ

An Hachette UK Company
www.hachette.co.uk
www.hachettechildrens.co.uk

Beast Quest®

Blaze
The
Ice Dragon

BY ADAM BLADE

ORCHARD

THE FORBIDDEN LAND

THE DEAD VALLEY

THE DEAD JUNGLE

THE DARK WOOD

THE DEAD PEAKS

CONTENTS

All hail, fellow followers of the Quest.

We have not met before, but like you, I have been watching Tom's adventures with a close eye. Do you know who I am? Have you heard of Taladon the Swift, Master of the Beasts? I have returned – just in time for my son, Tom, to save me from a fate worse than death. The Dark Wizard, Malvel, has stolen something precious from me, and until Tom is able to complete another Quest, I must wait between worlds, neither human nor ghost. I am half the man I once was and only Tom can return me to my former glory.

Will Tom have the strength of heart to help his father? This new Quest would test even the most determined hero. And there may be a heavy price for my son to pay if he defeats six more Beasts...

All I can do is hope – that Tom is successful and that I will one day be restored to full strength. Will you put your power behind Tom and wish him well? I know I can count on my son – can I count on you, too? Not a moment can be wasted. As this latest Quest unfolds, much rides upon it.

We must all be brave.

Taladon

PROLOGUE

Cries of pain drifted from the open door of the hut, but Derlot hurried on past towards the herb garden. He was one of the lucky ones – the terrible sickness had spared him so far. When the first shepherd had fallen sick from a hyena bite, no one in Rokwin had dreamt that the disease would spread. Derlot had been away at the market in Stonewin for two days, but by the time he returned the illness had touched almost every family in Rokwin. People were dying. Derlot just hoped that it was still in his power to help.

His father had been a medicine man who claimed that one of his herbs, horn-fern, could cure any sickness in Avantia.

Derlot unlatched the gate to the herb garden and picked his way over the plants. Many of the herbs were withered and the weeds grew tall. But then he saw it – the horn-fern, its dark green leaves tipped with red.

Derlot stooped among the plants and took out his pruning knife. The blade was poised against the herb's stalk, when a howling sound cut through the still summer air. Was that more hyenas?

Derlot stood up and looked around. Something was coiling through the trees towards him – a strange, dark shape, like smoke trailing from a campfire.

Derlot felt his mouth drop open in surprise. The shape was some kind of dragon, but not the type described in children's tales. Green and red scales covered the creature's snake-like body. Its long tail swayed back and forth, propelling it through the air and it opened its jaws to reveal vicious fangs.

Derlot stumbled backwards towards the open garden gate, but tripped and landed on the path. The dragon hovered in the air above him, as it opened its mouth, Derlot threw his hands up

to protect himself – he knew what
was coming.

Fire.

Suddenly a blast of freezing air
enveloped him. He lowered his hands
and saw that the garden had changed.
All the plants – including the precious
horn-fern – were locked in ice. The
ground at his feet was white with
frost, and even the laces of his boots
had frozen solid. The dragon had
breathed ice.

The creature hung lower in the sky,
and Derlot was pinned by its gaze.
There was something strange about
its green eyes – something almost
human. Was this a Beast or a man? Or
some terrible mixture of the two?

The dragon whipped its tail onto the

ground and
the earth shook with
the impact. Then the icy
fragments became mist, blinding
Derlot. As it cleared, he saw the
dragon flying towards the volcano
in Stonewin.

Derlot surveyed the ruins of the
garden and gave a low wail of despair.
Without his herbs, the villagers in
Rokwin were doomed.

And as for the people of Stonewin,
they had their own terrors to face.

1

LEAVING THE FORBIDDEN LAND

The sun was just a finger's breadth over the horizon as Tom and Elenna left the Dark Wood. Tom was tired. The battle with Luna the Moon Wolf had tested him to the limit – and Elenna, too.

"Perhaps we should rest," she suggested.

Tom glanced at his friend. Her

knees were scuffed from where she'd stumbled and fallen earlier.

He then looked at their brave animal companions. Silver, Elenna's wolf, trotted on ahead with his head low, and Tom's horse, Storm, staunchly plodded forwards.

"I wish we could," Tom said regretfully. "But not yet."

He fingered the leather thong around his neck, from which hung the pieces of the Amulet of Avantia. So far he'd retrieved four amulet parts and defeated each of the Ghost Beasts that had guarded them. But his Quest would not be complete until he had all six pieces, and the amulet was whole again. Only then would he be able to bring his father,

Taladon, back for good.

His next Quest, so his father had told him, was to defeat a dragon called Blaze.

"Well, we need to stop and check the map," said Elenna. "We can drink some water at the same time."

Tom nodded and sat down on a boulder. Elenna took a flask from Storm's saddlebag and drank, while Tom stretched out his hand in front of him.

"Map!" he commanded.

The air rippled as the ghostly map appeared. Without this gift from Aduro, they would never have been able to find their way through the Forbidden Land or locate the Beasts.

The map showed a glowing line,

like a thread of gold, snaking from where they stood at the edge of the Dead Wood, across the eastern fields, past a small village called Rokwin, and towards the town of Stonewin. It ended on the slopes of the volcano.

"Stonewin is where Epos lives," said Elenna, handing Tom the flask.

"I hope she's not in danger from this dragon," said Tom, taking a swig of water. Epos the Flame Bird was their loyal friend; on another occasion they had saved her from Dark Wizard Malvel.

Tom placed a hand over his eyes and gazed in the direction of Stonewin. He called on the power to see across great distances given to him by the golden helmet, part of the

suit of magical Golden Armour he
had retrieved.

"There's the volcano at Stonewin,"
he said to Elenna. "But the crater
isn't smoking. The volcano has
smoked since the day I was born.
Something's wrong."

"Then let's not waste any more
time," Elenna insisted.

Now Tom had seen their Quest

set out on the ghost map, strength returned to his heart, and they sped towards Avantian soil. As if sensing his urgency, Storm and Silver seemed to find new reserves of energy.

But even though his determination to complete the Quest was as strong as granite, worry tugged at Tom's mind. Each time he defeated one of Malvel's Ghost Beasts, one of his Golden Armour powers vanished. Now he only had two left.

Tom shook his head. The people of Stonewin, and maybe even Epos herself, needed him. He would not let them down. He would not let Malvel win.

Tom and Elenna reached the high wall that separated the Forbidden

Land from Avantia. They passed
silently through the unmanned gate,
back into familiar territory.

"I'd forgotten that the sky could
be so blue and the land so green,"
said Elenna. Storm whinnied and
wheeled about, bolting off across the
lush grass. Silver spun round in wild
circles of joy.

"If we don't succeed in this Quest,"
said Tom, "Malvel's Beasts will take
over Avantia, too – *everywhere* will
be as dead-looking as the Forbidden
Land."

"We won't let that happen," said
Elenna.

A fork of lightning suddenly split
the sky, which had rapidly darkened.

"The Forbidden Land may be

behind you," Malvel's voice rumbled thunderously above their heads, "but the curse of the Ghost Beasts is still strong. Four you have faced, but the Beast to come will be your end. No mortal can survive the dragon's breath."

"I do not fear Blaze!" shouted Tom.

Malvel laughed again. "Blaze will not be your only enemy this time.

You will face two adversaries as one."

The storm ended as quickly as it had begun, and Malvel was gone.

"Two adversaries!" said Elenna. "What does he mean?"

"I don't know," said Tom grimly. "But I'm not afraid to find out."

2

A LAND OF ICE

Tom and Elenna mounted Storm and galloped across the Avantian plain, Silver streaking beside them. Soon they were deep inside the kingdom, making good progress towards Stonewin.

Tom scanned the road ahead for danger, but to his surprise they saw no one at all. There weren't even any sheep grazing on the plains.

Tom slowed Storm to a canter, and once they were on the grass, he vaulted off his horse and crouched to inspect the ground.

"There's frost on this grass!"

Elenna frowned. "But it's summer."

Tom shrugged and remounted Storm. They continued their journey, passing lush green fields and bushes heavy with berries. A short while later they came to a pond, and Tom guided Storm and Silver over to the water for a well-earned drink. But as they approached the edge, he saw that the surface was frozen over.

"This is no ordinary cold weather, Elenna," he said. "Some places are green and alive, while a few paces away the ground is frozen solid."

Using the base of his shield, Tom
smashed a hole in the ice so that
Storm and Silver could drink.

"How can that be?" said Elenna.
"Stonewin's volcano has always
made the surrounding areas warmer
than usual, not colder."

They raced on. Soon, though, they came to a path that was covered with a great swathe of ice.

"We'll have to go slower," Tom told Elenna. "We can't risk injuring Storm on the slippery ground."

Picking their way carefully down the path, they passed a copse of trees bejewelled with frost and saw stone walls covered with ice.

Soon they came upon a signpost. One arm pointed towards Errinel, Tom's home village, and the other to Rokwin, which he knew was on the way to Stonewin.

"Let's hope we meet someone who can tell us what's going on," said Tom.

But he soon saw that the road

towards Rokwin was deserted
as well.

"People should be trading along
this route," said Elenna. "Where is
everyone?"

Tom shared her bemusement. Even
in the worst of weather the people of
Avantia went about their business.

Tom heard a noise coming from
ahead. Something was approaching
from around the bend in the road.
His hand fell to his sword hilt. Wild
animals roamed Avantia, and he
wouldn't be caught off guard. Elenna
had already unhooked her bow.

"Ready?" she asked, fixing an
arrow in place.

Tom nodded and held Storm's reins
a bit tighter.

A mare trotted around the corner, steered by her rider, who lay close against her back.

Tom breathed a sigh of relief and let go of his sword. "Stop there! I need to talk to you."

But the horse didn't slow.

"Stop. Please!" Tom guided Storm to stand sideways across the path.

The horse drew up in front of them. Its rider was slumped in the saddle, and only now turned his head slowly towards them. Tom recoiled when he saw the scabs covering the man's face.

Silver let out a whine of unease.

"Are you all right?" Elenna asked the man.

"Go back," the man whispered.

"Rokwin is doomed."

With those words, his eyes closed and he slipped from the saddle like a sack of grain. Tom could see that he was dead before he hit the ground. Silver took a few nervous steps towards the body, while Elenna got ready to dismount.

"No!" said Tom, guiding Storm between the man and the wolf.

"What's wrong?" said Elenna.

"For all we know, this man died of

something contagious," Tom replied. "We mustn't touch him."

Tom steered along the edge of the path, as far as the bend in the road. There he dismounted and used his magical sight to look into the town of Rokwin. No smoke issued from the chimneys of the houses, and no one walked the streets.

A flash of movement caught his eye. Behind a large storehouse, a crowd of townspeople had gathered. But something was wrong. They walked in aimless circles, bumping into each other and falling over.

Their faces were like the dead rider's – pale, with oozing sores. Some awful disease had infected the whole village.

With a troubled heart, Tom walked
back to Elenna.

"What did you see?" she asked.

He told her the fate of the
unfortunate villagers and she
gasped. "What can we do for them?"

"First, we have to find whatever
has caused this horror," said Tom.
*And make sure the same thing
doesn't happen to us,* he thought to
himself. His Quest had just become
twice as hard.

3

AMBUSHED

"Perhaps I can help them," said Elenna. "My uncle taught me how to use herbs as medicine."

Tom shook his head. "You can't, Elenna. You might become infected too."

"I'm not just leaving them, Tom," she replied hotly. "What about Epos's talon?"

Tom looked at the golden talon

embedded in his shield, a reminder of his last visit to Stonewin, when he had freed the Good Beast from Malvel's evil spell. The talon's healing powers had helped him many times, but this was different.

"The talon works on cuts and bruises," he explained. "The green jewel I took from Skor the Winged Stallion heals broken bones... But this is an illness – a *disease*. There's nothing we can do. We must focus on our Quest, and hope there's time to help afterwards."

Tom saw Elenna clench her fist with frustration. He put a hand on her shoulder and she ducked her head sadly.

"Is there another route to

Stonewin?" she asked after a moment, her voice hoarse.

Tom summoned his map again, and studied its shimmering surface.

"We can skirt the lower reaches of Rokwin, instead of going directly through it," he said, pointing to a thin line on the map. "Behind the forest there."

They set off on their new route and found it was deserted as well. Soon Rokwin dipped out of sight behind a bank of tall trees. Elenna was quiet as they rode and Tom could tell that, like him, she felt guilty at leaving the suffering villagers behind.

The road gradually became rougher, the ground covered in loose rocks and hidden dips. Silver scouted the way, nose to the floor, guiding them onwards. But he stopped as he came to a felled tree that blocked the path.

Tom halted Storm.

"The locals must have been cutting down trees for timber," said Elenna. "The illness meant that they had to stop work."

"Or they blocked the road on purpose," said Tom.

The fallen trunk was as wide as he was tall. Skirting the fallen tree would be almost impossible, as the path was narrow and the land bordering them on either side was sheer and rocky.

"We'll have to turn back," said Elenna.

"We can't," Tom replied. "There's no other way to Stonewin." He patted Storm's neck. "What do you think, boy? Think you can clear that trunk?"

Storm tossed his mane, and stamped his front hooves. Tom knew he could always rely on his horse's bravery.

"Hold on tight," he said to Elenna, and she gripped his waist.

Tom dug his heels into Storm's flank and the stallion bolted forwards, his hooves scattering rocks everywhere. As the fallen trunk loomed, Tom lifted the reins and gripped Storm's sides with his knees. Suddenly they were airborne and he felt his weight slam back in the saddle.

Storm's hooves cleared the bark by a finger's breadth, landing with a jolt on the other side. "Well done!" cried Tom, patting the horse's neck. He looked back and saw Silver scramble to the top of the trunk and stand there, panting.

"Catch your breath, boy," Tom called to the wolf. "You deserve—"

Something whizzed past Tom's ear – something fast and hot. He saw Silver spring away from the trunk and into the trees ahead.

"Take cover!" shouted Elenna.

Tom dragged Storm's reins around as a flare of light appeared between the trees ahead.

A flaming arrow.

The blazing shaft shot from the cover of the forest. In a moment, Tom's shield was on his arm and raised in defence. The arrow buried itself in his shield with a thud.

Then dozens of orange lights were visible in the forest, all illuminating angry faces.

Elenna sprang from Storm and Tom vaulted out of the saddle. He hit Storm's rear with his shield. "Go!" he shouted.

Storm bolted into the trees just as a hail of flaming arrows descended. Tom dragged Elenna behind him and threw up his shield. The arrows bounced off it.

The volley ended, but someone shouted, "Fire again!"

Tom held up one hand, showing the archers he was not a threat. "We mean you no harm," he shouted. "We're on a mission of peace."

Some muttering followed, and a voice called back, "Then turn around and go. You're not welcome here."

"We must get to Stonewin,"

Tom said. "The main road is filled with sickness."

"There's no sickness here, boy. We mean for it to stay that way."

Tom suddenly understood the reason behind their attack and took the risk of lowering his shield. A row of desperate faces looked back at him.

"This is our only option," said Tom. "Please...let us through. We're not sick."

One of the men stepped out of the trees, his bow down but the string taut with a loaded arrow. "Come forwards, then," he said. "Both of you."

Side by side, Tom and Elenna cautiously drew within ten paces of the group. Tom felt his confidence returning. Now that he wasn't being shot at, he could reason with these people. Show them that he wasn't a threa—

The ground beneath him suddenly seemed to rise up, and Tom and Elenna were lifted off their feet and pulled into the air. They were caught in some sort of net hanging from a tree.

It was a trap!

Beside him, Elenna gave a scream of rage and fear and began to struggle against the net. Tom's eyes focused on the man below, who pointed his arrow straight up at them.

This time there was no escape.

4

A VILLAGE IN NEED

The bowman's hand – poised to release the bowstring – shook with nerves.

Tom struggled to right himself in the net, but his legs kept slipping through the gaps.

"Don't shoot," Tom implored. "Look at us – we're not sick."

"We can't risk it," said a voice from the woods. "Kill them."

"Very well," said the archer, holding

the bow more firmly.

A scuffling sound came from the trees. Tom saw the man's eyes drop to his right and his mouth gape in surprise. Silver suddenly leapt from the shadows and sank his teeth into the man's arm. He screamed and dropped the bow and arrow.

Their enemy distracted, Tom managed to draw his sword and hack at the net.

"Hold onto me," he shouted to Elenna, and he felt her grip his waist. As the net fell open, he clutched one of the ropes with one hand, and the two friends swung out towards the archers, who were still among the trees. Tom let go and they dropped onto their enemies.

Elenna was up in a flash, her hunting dagger at the throat of an elderly man. Tom rolled across the ground and pointed his sword at the chest of the injured archer. Silver came to stand at Tom's side.

"Lower your bows!" shouted Elenna, pressing the point of her knife against the old man's skin. Tom knew his friend would never harm an Avantian, but she was playing the role well.

He got to his feet, keeping his sword aimed at the injured archer. One by one, the flaming arrow-points were extinguished.

"Don't hurt him," said the elderly man. "He's only frightened, like the rest of us."

"We won't hurt anybody," said Tom. "We only want to talk."

Elenna released the man, who hobbled warily towards Tom. His eyes were dark from lack of sleep and his grey skin was like old parchment.

"My name is Derlot," he said.

"I come from the village of Rokwin."

"I know the place," said Tom.

Derlot's face clouded. "You wouldn't recognise it now. Disease has ravaged it." He waved his hand at the faces between the trees. "We're the only ones who escaped."

The *clop-clop* of Storm's hooves made Tom turn. His stallion came out of the shelter of the woods and walked to his side.

"Where are you and your companions heading?" asked Derlot.

"Stonewin," said Tom, cautiously. "We are trying to reach the volcano there."

Derlot's eyes widened and he lowered his voice. "If the volcano is your destination, you must know of another threat to Avantia."

"What do you mean?" Tom asked.

Derlot stepped closer. "The plague is not the only curse to afflict this land. There's a dragon, too!"

Elenna looked at Tom in surprise, but Tom kept his face expressionless. Aduro had told him to never, ever reveal the truth of his Quests to anyone.

"A dragon!" he said. "Do they really exist?"

"I saw it with my own eyes," said Derlot. "A dragon that breathes ice instead of fire. My herbs to cure the ill were destroyed because of him."

Tom and Elenna shared a look. Did this explain the frozen ponds and icicles on the trees? Was Blaze responsible?

"If you don't believe me," said Derlot, "I can show you my herb garden. I just hope the dragon doesn't return."

Tom nodded. "Let's go."

Derlot guided them through the dense forest. Tom led Storm and Elenna followed with Silver at her side.

"No one in the village believes me," said Derlot, stooping under a branch. "But I know what I saw."

As they got deeper among the trees,

slowly climbing the lower slopes of Rokwin, Tom noticed that the air was becoming colder.

Storm snorted and white clouds formed at his nostrils. Tom could see his own breath, too. They'd been travelling for some time, and Tom wondered if the old man was lost.

"Not far now," whispered Derlot, pulling his cloak more tightly around him.

They emerged into a clearing. Elenna gasped. Tom saw that the ground was white with frost and crystals of ice glittered like tiny diamonds on the tips of broken stalks and ruined shrubs.

"This was the herb garden," said Derlot, "and my only hope of curing the sickness that afflicts my people."

"Poor thing!" said Elenna, pointing to a rabbit among the ice-encrusted plants. It was frozen mid-jump, its ears sticking up and its body stretched out as it had tried to flee. This was surely more than just unseasonably cold weather.

Silver sniffed at the frozen rabbit, then turned his head to Elenna, as if confused that his prey was not running away.

"Do you believe me now?" asked Derlot. "About the dragon?"

Tom nodded, feeling a chill in his heart that had nothing to do with the freezing cold air. "I believe you," he said.

This time Malvel and his Beasts had gone too far.

5

THE HYENAS OF ROKWIN

As they left the cold clearing behind, Elenna fell in step beside Derlot. "How was the sickness caused?" she asked.

"Five days ago," Derlot said, "one of the shepherds, Adam, was attacked and bitten by a hyena in the dark. He only managed to escape by beating the animal off with his staff and then climbing a tree."

Elenna held out her arm to help Derlot across a narrow stream.

"A hyena?" Tom exclaimed.

"Yes," Derlot continued. "It was strange because they don't normally come so close to Rokwin." The old man sighed. "Adam became sick in the night, sweating and mumbling in his sleep. By the next morning, the nurse looking after him was beginning to show signs of the same illness."

"It was spreading?" asked Tom, guiding Storm through a collection of boulders.

Derlot nodded. "The following dusk brought more hyenas. A dozen of them made a home in the thickets on the south side of the village. Their howls kept everyone awake. We posted archers and slingers around Rokwin's fences, but under the full moon they attacked." Derlot shook his head mournfully. "They sneaked into houses and bit whoever they could find."

"Did they kill many people?" asked Elenna.

"That's the strange thing," said Derlot. "It was almost as though these hyenas hadn't come to kill. They would bite only once, and then slip away back to their den in the thickets. By the morning, half of the village was ill. Those who weren't decided to flee…"

This sounds like Malvel's magic,

Tom thought. *Maybe the hyenas are the second adversary the Dark Wizard spoke of.*

When they reached the path again, it was almost dusk and the other villagers were waiting.

Elenna took Tom aside, while Derlot went to talk with his followers.

"Tom, we have to help these people," she whispered. "Even if it means delaying the Quest."

"You're right," he said. "I think Malvel is behind this, and we have to fight him wherever he appears. But what can we do about the plague?"

Elenna frowned for a moment, and then her face lit up. "My aunt always taught me that powdered willow bark was good for animal bites. Perhaps it'll work here, too."

"Do you have any?" Tom asked.

Elenna shook her head. "But the villagers may know where to find some."

She turned to the frightened group and asked them if any willow trees grew nearby.

"Down by the river," replied a stout young woman. "It's a fair walk, but the trees are plentiful."

As Elenna gathered the villagers to head to the riverbank, Tom jumped onto Storm.

"Where are you going?" asked Derlot.

"To deal with the hyenas," said Tom. "They're on the south side of the village, you say?"

"Yes," said Derlot, "but there are many. A boy like you will be torn to pieces."

Tom smiled. "I've faced hyenas before. They don't frighten me." He saw that Elenna was ready to go. "Be careful," Tom warned her. "There may be hyenas by the river, too."

Elenna crouched beside her wolf.

"I have Silver to look after me." She stroked the thick hair behind his neck. "You're not scared of a few mangy hyenas, are you?"

Silver growled and bared his teeth. Tom felt much better knowing that the wolf was at his friend's side.

He spurred Storm into action and galloped off along the road towards Rokwin.

Night was falling and every sound was magnified in Tom's ears. On either side the forest pressed down upon him. Owls seemed to hoot in welcome as he passed the outskirts of the village of Rokwin.

Soon the road disappeared, and Tom found himself surrounded by thorny bushes. *This must be the thicket Derlot meant,* he thought. Storm slowed, tossing his head with a whinny. Tom stroked the horse's mane and slipped off his back. There were tracks on the ground made by large pawprints – hyenas.

Low growls came from the thicket.

"Stay here," Tom whispered to

Storm, and set off in a crouch, following the sound. The sinister laughter of hyenas drifted over the night air as Tom crept between the sharp thorny branches. Then he saw them.

A pack of mangy creatures, their ribs showing through their hides, were fighting in a clearing. Grass

and dust flew up as they tore at each
other with their teeth and claws.
Saliva drooled from their jaws, and
they howled and gnashed their teeth.
Tom counted them: ten altogether.
He would have to form a plan so he
could fight them all at once.

Tom felt his nose twitch. A rank
smell, like rotten meat, had filled his

nostrils. Then he heard a tiny shuffle nearby. Tom twisted, drawing his sword just in time as a snarling hyena leapt from behind him. He thrust his sword towards the animal and it died on his blade. With his foot, Tom pushed the dead creature off his weapon.

The growls from the clearing had stopped. Tom looked up.

Ten pairs of eyes were on him, like twenty silver coins glittering in the moonlight. One by one, the hyenas loped forwards.

Then they broke into a run, coming straight for Tom. There was death in their eyes.

A NIGHT ATTACK

Tom knew he couldn't face all the
hyenas at once, and he sprinted back
towards Storm. He no longer had
the ability from the Golden Armour
to jump great distances, so he threw
himself onto Storm's saddle. The
hyenas surrounded him.

"Go!" he yelled, kicking his
stallion's sides. Storm charged
straight through the hyenas, causing

them to scatter. One yelped as it was trampled beneath the stallion's hooves.

The other hyenas regrouped and howled into the night, flashing their long yellow fangs.

A plan formed in Tom's head, but he'd have to make the hyenas follow him for it to work. Storm reared on his hind legs in alarm as the scavenging animals came closer, but Tom calmed him down.

"It's all right, boy," he said. "We're going to get out of this."

The hyenas paced back and forth, arching their spines, the hair on their necks standing straight up.

Again, Tom rode Storm directly at the mangy creatures. One leapt

up, but he swiped at it with the flat
of his sword. The others dodged
aside, their thin black lips curled
into snarls.

Tom galloped back along the
road, past Rokwin and through the
forest. Behind him he could hear
the yapping of the hyenas as they
pursued him. They were close.

Storm charged between the trees fearlessly, the branches whipping at Tom's face.

A bank of solid trunks blocked the path and Tom changed direction. Two hyenas moved quickly through the undergrowth and threw themselves at Storm's flank. Tom let go of the reins to beat one away with his shield, stabbing at the other.

Storm burst through the far side of the forest. They were out in the fields again, heading back towards the Forbidden Land. Storm was soaked with sweat, and his mane streamed in the darkness, but he galloped on.

When it seemed they were pulling away from the hyenas, Tom slowed his horse down to keep their pursuers in the chase. He couldn't afford to lose them now. Not when his plan was nearly complete.

They passed the frozen pond where he and Elenna had re-entered Avantia and then plunged back into the Dark Wood. It had been the location of his previous Quest, against Luna the Moon Wolf. Tom steered Storm along the complicated

paths that led between the trees.
It was as if they'd been etched into
his brain. The yellow jewel he won
defeating Narga the Sea Monster had
given him a perfect memory.

As they threaded between the bare
silvered trunks, the padding of the
hyenas' paws behind them grew
softer. Tom risked a look back, and
saw only four or five of the creatures
slinking through the shadows.

They looked uncertain. His ruse
had worked: the hyenas were
disorientated and in unfamiliar
territory. And several of them were
already lost in the forest.

Tom's legs ached from gripping
Storm's flanks, but he did not
slacken his hold. He criss-crossed

the woods until the last of the hyenas fell to the ground, its tongue lolling from its exhausted mouth. Then Tom galloped away, leaving it deep in the maze of dark trees. With any luck, none of the hyenas would return to spread disease ever again.

It was the middle of the night when Tom and Storm trotted back down the forest path towards Rokwin.

Grey smoke curled into the sky from the small fires that lit the outskirts of the village. The uninfected villagers he'd seen in the forest were huddled at the firesides, boiling a foul-smelling broth in iron pots. Tom found Elenna beside one. Silver lay patiently at her feet.

"You're back!" she said.

Tom slipped from Storm's back. "The hyenas will no longer be a problem."

"We've been busy here as well.

We found the willow bark," Elenna said, and they walked to where two thin and bedraggled women were sleeping soundly. Another was sitting up, sipping from a wooden cup.

"These three women were sick only a few hours ago."

Tom smiled through his weariness.

"Your friend is very skilled," said a voice he recognised. Tom saw Derlot coming towards them. "We've enough medicine to heal everyone. Soon the whole of Rokwin will be cured."

Tom was happy, but he couldn't

allow himself to relax. One obstacle was overcome, but Malvel's Beast still awaited them.

"We should go," he said.

"No!" exclaimed Derlot. "We must give you a feast. You have both saved our lives."

"I'm afraid we have another problem to deal with," said Tom. "And it cannot wait."

"The dragon?" Derlot whispered.

Tom nodded, unable to lie. He climbed onto Storm, and helped Elenna up behind him. "Goodbye, Derlot," he said.

"Farewell, young heroes," the old man replied. The villagers cheered and waved them off, shouting their thanks.

Storm galloped along the rocky path towards Stonewin, Silver at his side, and soon the crackle of the villagers' fires and the smell of wood-smoke were far behind.

When he saw the volcano rise up ahead in the distance, Tom felt as though he was returning home. He smiled to himself as he remembered the last time he had visited this place – on his Quest to free Epos. Back then, the sight of the gigantic flame bird with her blazing feathers had filled him with dread. But once rescued from Malvel's spell, Epos had become one of his most loyal friends.

Tom frowned. The volcano had lost its bitter smell of sulphur and the air wasn't as warm as it should have been. It was as if the great volcano had become dormant and sapped of life.

Using his magical sight, Tom scoured the slopes for Malvel's fifth Ghost Beast. Nothing stirred in the darkness. "We should stop for the night," he said. "We can look for Blaze when the sun rises."

Elenna seemed happy to rest, and lay with Silver in the shelter of a large boulder. Storm lounged by the side of the path and Tom sat against his soft underbelly, determined to keep his eyes open in case danger approached.

His mind returned to Epos. Was the flame bird in danger? If Malvel had harmed her, Tom vowed that his revenge would be swift. But his anger didn't keep him awake. The stars began to drift in front of his eyes, and he felt sleep envelop him.

He woke with a start. An icy feeling pressed against his chest.

Tom looked down and saw something moving across his torso. His hands touched the green and red scales, thick as saddle leather, which coiled around him.

Blaze!

1

A FAMILIAR FOE

Panic and pain choked Tom's throat as the dragon's length tightened around him. He tried to stand up, but he couldn't move his legs. The dragon had looped its snaky form around his lower body. Two gleaming eyes set in a narrow head on a long neck swung round to look straight at him.

Tom stared as a forked tongue, black as night, flickered in and out between the Beast's bloodless reptilian lips. The dragon brought its head right up to Tom's face. Tom wanted to look away, but he couldn't. There was something about the dragon's eyes. They weren't like any Beast's he'd seen before. They looked…human. Tom was sure he'd seen them somewhere before.

He tried to call out to Elenna, but a thin wheezing sound was the only noise that came from his mouth. He writhed, attempting to push out his arms. He twisted his shoulders and jerked his hips – anything to loosen the dragon's death-hold. As if in response, the scaly body contracted and Tom felt his ribs begin to crack.

Storm snorted in the darkness

and Elenna slept on, a few paces away from Tom and oblivious to the danger. He had to wake her. If he died, she would be next. Tom saw his shield leaning up against a rock. If he could knock it over the sound might awaken Elenna.

As the Beast's muscular grip shifted again, Tom gasped as he tried to draw breath. The ice dragon's head didn't move – it was as if Blaze wanted to *watch* him suffocate. Then Tom realised where he had seen those eyes before.

Malvel!

Somehow the Dark Wizard was *inside* the Beast, controlling him with his evil magic.

With a mighty effort, Tom

stretched his leg towards the shield, managing to slip his foot behind it. Summoning the last vestiges of his strength, he flicked the shield up into the air and it clattered onto a small rock.

Elenna was on her feet in a heartbeat.

Tom's vision darkened and his limbs grew weak. Was this the end?

Suddenly Blaze's death-grip weakened and air filled Tom's lungs. He immediately saw the cause. One of Elenna's arrows was sticking out from the dragon's body. Silver charged forwards and tried to bite Blaze's side, but his teeth slid helplessly off the thick scales.

"Hold on!" Elenna shouted,

stringing another arrow to her bow. Tom wriggled free and rolled across the ground towards his sword. But before he could grab the hilt, the tentacle-like coil of Blaze's tail wrapped around his ankle. Tom looked over his shoulder and saw that he was being dragged towards the Beast's gaping jaws. The dragon's teeth were a chilly green, but his mouth was blood-red.

Tom pulled himself by his fingernails towards the sword, feeling his sinews stretch to their limit.

Finally, he locked his fingers around the hilt. As he was pulled backwards, he turned and swiped at the Beast's head. But the blade passed straight through the dragon and thwacked into the ground. Blaze's body was now see-through. He'd turned into a ghost!

Tom felt himself swell with rage as he got to his feet. Like the other Beasts on this Quest, Blaze had the ability to transform from a real to a ghostly form in an instant. Tom swung with his sword again, trying to hack at the semi-transparent scales, but once more his sword met no resistance and passed through the Beast. The colour rushed back into Blaze's body as he took on his flesh-and-blood form.

"Look!" shouted Elenna, pointing. "The amulet piece!"

Tom's heart thumped as he saw that the amulet fragment was lodged between the scales where Blaze's body met his head. Tom hopped onto a boulder and leapt towards the dragon, reaching for his prize.

The Beast lashed its tail out like a whip and Tom was struck in the chest and fell to the ground. He watched helplessly as the ice dragon took to the skies, climbing steadily through the air, his tail whipping out behind to thrust him upwards. Silver howled at the departing Beast while Storm neighed angrily.

Blaze hovered above the volcano's crater and Malvel's laughter boomed, shaking the slopes. "Come and catch me...if you dare." With those words, Blaze dipped his head and plunged into the heart of the crater.

Tom got to his feet.

"It sounds like a trap," said Elenna.

The first pale light of dawn was breaking. Tom realised they hadn't slept for long, but he wasn't tired. Coming so close to death had made him feel more alive than ever.

"We've outsmarted Malvel before –
we'll outsmart him again! We must
go after Blaze."

Tom saw Storm's legs twitch, as if
the horse was eager to start the day.

"You stay here, boy," said Tom.
"We should travel by foot on the
volcano."

Elenna stroked Silver. "And you
look after him," she said.

Waving goodbye to their animal
companions, Tom and Elenna set off
up the path. The cold air cut right
through them.

"Do you remember the last time
we were here?" asked Elenna, as
they climbed up the craggy rock
face. "Lava flowed down from the

crater edge."

Tom nodded as he scrambled onto a ledge. "The villagers would have lost their homes, but we succeeded in our Quest and saved Epos."

"Epos…" said Elenna, her voice grave. "Where is she? Why is it so cold up here?"

Tom looked up towards the crater, where Epos's nest was. So far he hadn't even felt her presence. His anger tightened like a knot inside him. "If Malvel has harmed my friend," he said, "he will pay."

1

EPOS IMPRISONED

The air grew even colder as they climbed up the winding path of the barren slopes. It was as though all the laws of nature had been turned upside down.

As they headed towards the crater's edge, the shrieking wind stung Tom's eyes and carried his breath away on icy currents. He looked over at Elenna, and saw that her lips had started to turn purple.

"Are you all right to go on?" he shouted above the wind.

"W-w-while I c-c-c-can still fire an arrow, I won't stop," she called back.

Pain throbbed in Tom's legs as he picked his way over the final yards to the edge of the crater. Long ago he'd watched Epos majestically rise from this very spot, her ruby-red feathers aflame and her talons dipped in gold. Where was she now?

Elenna reached his side, the wind lashing her hair across her pale face. They both peered into the chasm below.

Tom's heart filled with despair. The shallow sides of the crater were covered in crystals of ice.

Great blue-white columns rose up from the depths like towers of diamonds. The lava pool, which should have been bubbling at the bottom of the crater, was completely frozen over. And there, below the surface, was a sight that made Tom more despairing still. Epos, her mighty wings spread wide, was trapped under the ice shelf!

"Poor Epos!" gasped Elenna. "Only Malvel could be so cruel."

Tom was almost speechless with anger. "We have to rescue her!"

Blaze was nowhere to be seen, so they began to climb down the steep walls of the crater, placing each foot with care. Epos glided up to the roof of her frozen prison. A fireball like a miniature sun formed between her talons, and she hurled it against the ice shelf.

"She's trying to escape," said Elenna.

Epos did the same again, and this time Tom saw a crack appear in the frozen sheet. They reached the flatter ground by the frozen lava pool and watched as another of the flame bird's fiery orbs hit the ice, causing a second fissure to appear in the ice shelf.

"It's working," said Elenna.

"One more, Epos!" Tom urged. "You can do it!"

As the fourth fireball was growing between the flame bird's talons, a roar from above shook the walls of the volcano. Tom looked up. Blaze was diving towards them, his mouth open wide, razor teeth dripping with drool, and his human eyes glinting with ferocious intent. Malvel's cackle echoed around the crater.

The Beast swooped past them, a surge of icy air blasting from his jaws, which he directed over the ice shelf. Tom felt his heart sink – the frozen sheet was now twice as thick.

Epos's fireballs were having little effect on the toughened barrier, but still she tried, hurling ball after ball against the ice. Each time it looked as if her efforts might succeed, the Beast blew more freezing air to cut off her escape. Blaze seemed only interested in keeping Epos

imprisoned and paid no attention to
Tom and Elenna.

"There must be a way to stop
Blaze," said Elenna.

"We don't have to stop him," said Tom. "We just have to keep him busy and give Epos a chance to escape. Can you distract him long enough for me to get down to the ice shelf?"

Elenna had strung an arrow before the words were out of his mouth.

"Good," he said. "Get Blaze's attention."

Elenna loosed an arrow across the cavern at the dragon and Blaze shrieked in pain as it found its mark in his side. Tom began scrambling down to the ice, sliding over the slippery ground. He saw Elenna fire another arrow, but this time Blaze shifted into his ghost form and it passed straight through him.

Tom was now down on the ice.

Seeing him so close, Epos hurled another fireball at the shelf.

"Look out!" Tom heard Elenna call. He turned to see Blaze flying right at him. He dived aside as a blast of ice shot from the dragon's mouth. Tom sprang up and lunged at the Beast. He swung his sword as the dragon wheeled in the air, but at the last instant Blaze became a ghost and the blade passed through him. With another freezing blast, the dragon had reinforced the ice shelf.

How can I defeat this Beast? Tom wondered. *I can't even get near him!*

Undaunted, Epos lit another ball, the bright light shining through the ice and casting Tom's shadow onto the volcano's wall. Tom saw

Blaze coming at him again and he sprang up, trying to drive the point of his sword into the Beast's heart. Once more, Blaze assumed his ghostly form and the attack was in vain. The Evil Beast hovered, semi-transparent, just above Tom's head.

"Out of tricks?" Malvel's voice sneered.

Tom's anger took over, and he slashed his sword wildly at the air.

Out of the corner of his eye, Tom saw his shadow make the same movement, and to his surprise Blaze shrieked and writhed. It was as though the blade of Tom's shadow had somehow connected with the Ghost Beast. A fat drop of blue blood dripped from Blaze's scales.

Tom's eyes were drawn to Epos.

For some reason the flame bird was clutching a fireball, but hadn't thrown it. The light from the fireball meant that Tom cast a looming shadow on the wall. *Could it be…?* Yes, Epos was telling him something important.

Tom stabbed wildly again, and his shadow's blade connected with the Ghost Beast. Blaze roared with pain for a second time, confusion showing in his glinting eyes. But Tom wasn't confused – he now understood why Epos was holding the fireball. It made Tom's shadow permanent. His skin tingled as he realised what this meant.

I might not be able to fight the

Ghost Beast, he thought, *but my shadow can!*

SHADOW WARRIOR

Tom readied himself to strike again, but the Ghost Beast surged upwards, landing on an icy ledge out of the reach of Tom's shadow. Tom knew that he had to press his advantage while the Beast was stunned with his injuries, but how could he attack Blaze with his shadow while the Ghost Beast cowered far above him?

Of course, he thought. *The white*

jewel! He pulled the gem he had won from Kaymon the Gorgon Hound out of his belt. It gave him the power to separate himself from his shadow.

Tom climbed up to Elenna, who kept her bow trained on the ice dragon in case he shifted out of his ghostly form. He whispered in her ear so that Malvel wouldn't be able to hear his plan.

"My shadow is the only thing that can harm Blaze while he is in his ghost form," he said. "And the only way my shadow can reach him is if I use the jewel from Kaymon."

Elenna frowned. "It's too dangerous, Tom," she whispered back. "When your shadow is separated from you, your body can't move. You won't be able to defend yourself if Blaze comes after you."

Tom could see that she spoke out of worry for him, but he would not be swayed. "I know it's a risk," he said, "but if we wait here, Blaze will recover, and he'll freeze us just like that rabbit in Derlot's garden."

Suddenly Epos gave a tired-sounding cry and the fireball in her talons faded a little. Tom looked back at Elenna, whose face had hardened.

"I'll do my best to protect you," Elenna said. "If Blaze comes too close, I'll have my arrows ready."

Tom gave Elenna a quick hug of thanks, then took a deep breath, calling on the power of the white jewel.

Dizziness gripped his head, and he

put out a foot to steady himself before he opened his eyes.

But he hadn't moved.

"Tom," said Elenna excitedly. "It's working!"

One leg of his shadow had peeled away. Tom ordered the other leg to do the same, and his shadow stood beside him as though it were a whole other person. In his mind, Tom told it to unsheathe its sword. Though his own arms were as still as a statue, his shadow drew its blade.

Do battle with Blaze, he told it. Tom was powerless to move, but his shadow did exactly as he asked, darting across the ice and clambering up the far side of the cavern wall towards the ledge where Blaze was beginning to stir once again.

Quicker! Tom urged. His shadow rippled silently over the wall, and heaved itself onto the ledge.

The Ghost Beast immediately turned to face the shadow, striking out with his tail. The shadow ducked and countered with its blade, bringing out a bloodcurdling cry of agony from the ice dragon. Blaze leapt off the ledge and glided downwards, blowing another fresh layer of ice onto Epos's prison. Tom's shadow jumped down too, its sword held aloft, relentlessly chasing Blaze.

Why didn't Malvel's Beast stay and fight? Tom wondered. *Why was it so important to keep the ice shelf in place?*

Epos, lit another fireball, while Blaze and Tom's shadow faced off again. The Ghost Beast darted forwards, dodged the shadow's sword at the last moment, then flicked his muscular tail out. It struck Tom's shadow in the head, knocking him back against the wall. Tom felt the bruising pain as though his actual body had been hit.

But instead of going after the shadow, Blaze breathed another icy blast at Epos, refreezing the ice shelf.

Realisation dawned in Tom's mind. Blaze was an *ice dragon*. Epos was a *flame bird*. Just as ice could imprison Epos, what if *heat* was Blaze's enemy? Was that why Blaze was keeping Epos imprisoned?

Tom wished he could tell Elenna his theory - she might be able to help Epos break the ice. But he did not want to risk attracting Blaze's attention. No, he had to be smarter about this. Somehow, he would have to move.

His brain told him it was impossible, but his heart told him otherwise.

Tom sent his shadow running to the far side of the cavern, and Blaze followed. While they were busy, Tom channelled all his willpower into making his frozen limbs move. He felt a sweat break out all over his body, and his heart thundered in his chest. He managed to make his head turn, but it felt as though the sinews in his neck were being torn apart. Next he concentrated on moving his arm. It was like trying to lift the anvil in his uncle's forge. His body screamed with pain, but the arm finally moved a fraction. His eyes caught Elenna's expression – her mouth was wide open in amazement.

It took all his strength of heart, but somehow Tom dragged his body over to Epos's ice prison. He lifted his shield above his head. Beneath the ice, Epos flapped her wings madly in anticipation. The sight was enough to drive Tom on. With a growl of determination, he brought the shield down, ramming it into the ice.

A crack splintered the centre of the sheet and Tom fell to his knees. He watched with delight as Epos burst free in a shower of icy splinters and took to the air. The crater was suddenly filled with golden light and, all around, the ice began to melt and trickle in rivulets down the walls.

Malvel's cry of despair split the cavern, and Blaze suddenly became his solid form once again. Through the searing heat, the Beast's green and red scales glistened. It seemed Blaze couldn't remain a ghost in the midst of the smoking molten rock. The dragon hovered over Tom's shadow, but the solid Beast posed it no danger.

"You've done it!" cried Elenna. "Epos is free."

Despite this, Tom knew the Quest was far from over. He still couldn't move properly, and was vulnerable until his shadow returned to him. He knelt on the remains of the ice and called his shadow back.

But Blaze had already spotted him. The dragon turned its massive body and began flying in for the attack. Tom's shadow ran behind, but it wasn't as quick as the Beast.

As Blaze slithered through the
air towards him, Tom again saw
the amulet piece near the dragon's
shoulder – the amulet piece he needed
to bring his father back to his flesh
and blood form. Now he feared that
would never happen. The icy jaws
gaped, ready to devour him.

10

FACE TO FACE WITH MALVEL

Elenna's arrow thudded into Blaze's neck and the Beast veered off-course, smashing into the ground. The distraction gave Tom's shadow enough time to return to his body.

As Tom joined up with his shadow once more, power surged through him. He sprang to his feet. "Thanks, Elenna!" he called.

"Now finish off that Beast!" she yelled back.

"With pleasure," Tom muttered, seeing Blaze rise up. He couldn't use his ghostly form to escape any more.

Blaze's green eyes flashed. "You'll die in this volcano, Tom," said a voice. It was a roar, but the tone was Malvel's.

The dragon sent a jet of freezing air towards Tom. He threw himself out of the way, feeling the icy air brush his legs.

Epos swooped down and crashed into Blaze, her talons raking his skin. Tom saw something drop to the ground and land in the corner of the volcano, next to a bubbling chasm of lava.

The amulet fragment!

"Get the amulet piece!" Tom shouted to Elenna, as Blaze shook Epos loose and faced him again. The dragon released another jet of ice and Tom charged forwards, ducking beneath the icy stream and stabbing upwards with his sword. The blade lodged in the thick scales of the dragon's stomach and Tom lost his grip on the hilt as Blaze soared up into the air.

Looking over, Tom saw Elenna slip the precious amulet fragment inside her pocket, and he ran to her side.

Blaze whipped around to face them and stalked forwards, Tom's sword still hanging from his underside. Tom and Elenna found themselves right by the edge of a molten pool. There was nowhere they could go.

Epos cawed from above and descended to attack Blaze, but the dragon flicked his tail out and sent the flame bird spinning into the lava.

"I told you that you'd die here," screeched Malvel's voice.

Blaze arched his back and readied

himself to deliver the final attack. But instead of fear, Tom felt a strange calm. There was a way out of this predicament. He just had to outwit both the Beast and the Dark Wizard.

Tom took a few steps forward.

"What are you doing?" shouted Elenna. "You'll get yourself killed!"

"Stay back," said Tom. If Elenna was too close, his plan would fail.

White smoke appeared in Blaze's nostrils and the dragon opened his mouth to release his icy breath. Tom waited until the last possible moment, then lifted his shield as the blast shot forth. The freezing air hammered into it. Peering over the rim, Tom saw the flow of ice

rebounding off the shield's surface
and deflecting back at Blaze,
encasing him in ice. Tom held on,
even as the wood of his shield
started to creak. The air around him
was bitterly cold, but Nanook's bell,
which he had won when he freed the
snow monster, protected him.

Slowly, a thick icy barrier appeared
between Tom and Blaze, reaching
all the way out to the edge of the
volcano's wall.

Tom checked behind him, and
saw Elenna shivering with the cold.
Her teeth were chattering, but she
managed a smile. Tom was glad
she'd stayed back, any closer, and her
blood would have frozen.

Then she held a shaky arm out, and
pointed past him. "M…M…Malvel,"
she stuttered.

Tom turned back and saw the Dark
Wizard lying on the ground beside
the frozen Beast. The cold must have
driven him out of the dragon's body.
He climbed to his feet, shaking his
head in confusion, before catching

sight of Tom through the ice wall. He stepped forwards and ran his fingers over the cold surface, his eyes never leaving Tom's.

"Blaze is finished," Tom told Malvel. "And so are you."

The Dark Wizard smashed his fists against the wall.

"This isn't over!" he screamed. "I'll have my revenge!"

Tom ran at the wall, hoping to crash through it. A thin crack appeared. He wanted nothing more than to face his archenemy one-on-one.

But Malvel's mouth curled to a smirk, and he slowly backed away. "Another time, young adversary," he said. "Another time."

"While there's blood in my veins," shouted Tom, ramming the ice with his shoulder again, "I'll defeat you!"

Malvel's form seemed to drift out of the volcano wall, and Blaze faded away with him. The sword that had been lodged in the dragon's belly clattered to the ground.

Epos appeared by their side, her wings blazing with healthy flames.

A fireball hovered between her talons. Tom stepped back as the flame bird sent it spinning into the ice wall.

As the fire died, a hole appeared in the centre of the wall, melting outwards. When it was big enough, Tom and Elenna climbed through.

Tom knelt and picked up his sword.

"Malvel was so close to us," he said. "Almost close enough to touch."

"Don't worry, Tom," Elenna said. "At least we have this." She held up the amulet piece.

Tom took the fragment and joined it with the others that hung around his neck. As soon as he did so a light appeared before them, almost blinding in its brightness. And there, only a few paces away, was a ghostly shape he knew as well as his own reflection.

"Father!" Tom cried.

"You have triumphed once more, my son," said Taladon. "Epos is safe, and Malvel is driven back for now."

Tom longed to throw his arms around his father, but he knew it was impossible. Until he collected the sixth and final piece of the amulet, his father would remain a ghost.

"We only have one more Quest to go," said Tom. "Then you'll be flesh and blood again."

Taladon nodded slowly. "One last Quest, but a Quest deadlier than all those that have come before. Hold fast to your courage. You will need it."

With those words, he disappeared.

Tom longed to keep his father with him, but put his sadness from his mind.

On the other side of the ice wall, Epos spread her wings. "I think she's offering us a ride," said Elenna.

Tom climbed onto the flame bird's

back, and Elenna settled beside him.

The Beast leapt into the air, beat
her wings, and took them up through
the glowing crater. When they
emerged into the clear air of Avantia,
Tom heaved a sigh of relief. The frost
from the land had gone.

They dismounted Epos on

Stonewin's peak, and the flame bird dived back into the volcano.

Tom was pleased that he'd succeeded in his Quest, but he knew that Malvel's sorcery would not be kept at bay for long. And there was a sixth and final Beast to face.

"The end is close," Elenna said.

"One last push," he replied. *And I'll be ready when you come again, Malvel,* Tom thought. *I'll always be ready.*

CONGRATULATIONS, YOU HAVE COMPLETED THIS QUEST!

At the end of each chapter you were awarded a special gold coin. The QUEST in this book was worth an amazing 11 coins.

Look at the Beast Quest totem picture inside the back cover of this book to see how far you've come in your journey to become

MASTER OF THE BEASTS.

The more books you read, the more coins you will collect!

Do you want your own Beast Quest Totem?
1. Cut out and collect the coin below
2. Go to the Beast Quest website
3. Download and print out your totem
4. Add your coin to the totem
www.beastquest.co.uk/totem

Don't miss the next exciting Beast Quest book, STEALTH! THE GHOST PANTHER

Read on for a sneak peek...

CHAPTER ONE

EVIL IN THE CITY

Tom stood beside Elenna on the edge of the volcano at Stonewin and looked down at the piece of amulet that he held in the palm of his hand. The gold shone in the sunlight and

the piece of enamel glowed and winked like a blue eye.

"That's five pieces," he said. "Only one more to go."

Pulling on the leather thong around his neck, he fished the rest of the amulet out from under his tunic and fitted the new piece into place. Golden light flared briefly and when it died away the new piece had joined with the rest as if it had never been broken off. A jagged gap showed where the final piece was still missing.

"It won't be long now," Elenna said. "Then your father will be fully returned to his old self."

Tom nodded slowly. "But I've lost another of my special powers," he reminded his friend. "I haven't got the strength of heart from the golden chainmail anymore. And that helped me through so many of our Quests."

"You don't need it!" Elenna assured him. "You've got enough courage of your own."

Storm, Tom's black stallion, blew out a noisy breath as if he was agreeing, and Elenna's grey wolf, Silver, gave a long howl.

"See?" Elenna went on. "They know you're brave enough for anything! And so does your father."

Tom smiled at her, feeling a wave of determination fill his chest. His father, Taladon, had been captured by Malvel, the Dark Wizard. Although he had escaped when Tom defeated Malvel for the third time, he was trapped as a ghost between the real world and the spirit world. Taladon could only return to life when the six pieces of the Amulet of Avantia had been joined together again. But Malvel had given the pieces to six Ghost Beasts. Tom had already defeated five of the powerful monsters, but he still had to face the sixth. And he knew that this last Beast would be the deadliest of all.

"So where do we go next?" Elenna asked.

Tom stretched out one hand. "Map!" he commanded.

The ghostly map given to them by Wizard Aduro took shape in front of him, bobbing gently in the air.

A shimmering path appeared, leading from the volcano to the main city of Avantia.

"That's where King Hugo's palace is!" Elenna exclaimed. "Surely the Ghost Beast wouldn't dare go there?"

"I don't know." A cold sense of approaching evil crept through Tom. "Maybe that's what my father meant when he said the next Beast would be closer to home."

"And more evil than we can possibly know," Elenna added. "It must be really cunning to have hidden itself in the very heart of Avantia – let alone to go near King Hugo and Wizard Aduro."

Tom felt his hands ball into fists.

"I don't care how cunning it is.

We'll defeat it!"

Beside the picture of the city a small black shape came into view: a panther with a coat the colour of night. It snarled at Tom as he gazed at it, and slid out gleaming claws.

At the same moment a chilly wind blew past Tom, bringing the foul stench of something rotten. The voice of evil Wizard Malvel whispered in Tom's ear. "Stealth…"

"Stealth!" Elenna exclaimed; clearly she had heard the whisper too. She exchanged a startled glance with Tom. "Is that the name of the Ghost Beast?"

"It must be," Tom declared. "And we were right. The Beast is in The City."

"And that means it's not just our own safety we have to worry about," Elenna said. "The king and everyone else are in danger too."

Tom's stomach churned with a mixture of fear and excitement. "We'd better get moving," he said. "This Beast could destroy the whole of Avantia."

Read
STEALTH THE GHOST PANTHER
to find out more!

FIGHT THE BEASTS, FEAR THE MAGIC

Are you a BEAST QUEST mega fan?
Do you want to know about all the latest news,
competitions and books before anyone else?

Then join our Quest Club!

Visit the BEAST QUEST website
and sign up today!

www.beastquest.co.uk

Discover the new Beast Quest mobile game fron

Available free on iOS and Android

Guide Tom on his Quest to free the Good Beasts
of Avantia from Malvel's evil spells.

Battle the Beasts, defeat the minions,
unearth the secrets and collect
rewards as you journey through the
Kingdom of Avantia.

DOWNLOAD THE APP TO BEGIN
THE ADVENTURE NOW!